WHEE!

Collect all the Preston Pig Stories

Colin McNaughton
Suddenly!

Colin McNaughton
GOAL!

Colin McNaughton
BOO!

Colin McNaughton
Shh!
(Don't Tell Mister Wolf)
A Preston Pig Lift-the-Flap Book

Colin McNaughton
Oops!

Colin McNaughton
Hmm...
A Preston Pig Story

Colin McNaughton
Oomph!
A Preston Pig Story

Coming soon!

First published in Great Britain by HarperCollins Publishers in 2001

1 3 5 7 9 10 8 6 4 2

ISBN: 0 00 712371 X

From the television series based on the original Preston Pig books created, written and illustrated by Colin McNaughton
Text © Colin McNaughton/HarperCollins Publishers Ltd 2001
Illustrations in this work derived from the television series © Colin McNaughton/Varga-London Ltd 1999

Production of the television series by Varga-London Ltd and Link Entertainment; Licensed by Link Licensing Ltd
The author/illustrator asserts the moral right to be identified as the author/illustrator of the work.
A CIP catalogue record for this title is available from the British Library.

The HarperCollins website address is: www.fireandwater.com

Printed in Hong Kong

Colin McNaughton
WHEE!

Collins

An imprint of HarperCollinsPublishers

Preston is playing football in the park when his friend, Pumpkin, rides up on her bike.

"Look, Preston!" gasps Pumpkin, waving a poster. "It's the annual Hot Trotters Skateboard competition this afternoon. There's prizes and everything!"

Billy the Bully stomps by and snatches the poster.

"Don't even think about it, squirt!" says Billy the Bully. "With me in that competition, you don't stand a chance!"

"Pumpkin, let's go and get my skateboard!" says Preston.

Nearby, Mister Wolf
has been listening.
"Hmm...Hot Trotters!"
says Mister Wolf.
"Yum, yum! I like the
sound of that! I'll have
to get some
wheels too!"

Preston's mum and dad are in the garden.
"Those are your best flowers yet," says
Preston's mum.

"Yes," says Preston's dad. "I'll get first
prize at the flower show
with these."

After they go indoors Preston comes hurtling, out of control, down the path on his skateboard.

Guess where the flowers land?

Preston's dad steps out of the house and sees Mister Wolf.

"Er…um…I can explain!" whimpers Mister Wolf.

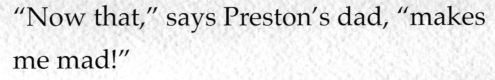

"Now that," says Preston's dad, "makes me mad!"

Thump! Mister Wolf sails out of the garden and lands in a passing rubbish lorry.

"That hurt!" says Mister Wolf.

Whee!

Preston is practising.

"Ow! Ouch! Yow!" says Preston.

"That's pathetic, Preston!" says Pumpkin.

"What you need is a coach."

Mister Wolf is also practising.

Whee!

Crash!
Bang!

Mister Wolf lands in a rubbish bin.

"That really hurt!" says Mister Wolf.

Pumpkin does her best to help Preston but he's still not very good.

"Come on," says Pumpkin, "we have to go. The competition is about to begin."

The crowds cheer. The music plays. One by one the competitors show off their skills. At last, it's Preston's turn…

Meanwhile, at the bottom of the hill, Mister Wolf is pushing a huge pot of carrots and onions into place under the skateboard ramp. "Yum, yum!" says Mister Wolf.

Just as Preston is about to go, Billy the
Bully shoves past him.

"Watch the master at work!" says Billy
the Bully and he hurtles off down the hill…

Guess where he lands?

"Oh…er…um…I can explain," says Mister Wolf.

"Oi! Wolf! Come 'ere!" says Billy the Bully.

Thump!

Whee!

Preston sets off.

"Go, Preston, go!"

says Pumpkin.

Mister Wolf lands on the back of Preston's skateboard. Preston flips into the air…

…and lands on Mister Wolf's head.

"Aaaaaarrrrrrghh!" yells Mister Wolf.

"Aaaaaarrrrrrghh!" yells Preston.

Preston ends up winning first prize.

Mister Wolf ends up in the rubbish lorry.

"Preston! Preston! He's the best 'un!" chants the crowd.

"My hero," says Pumpkin.

"Sausages!" says Mister Wolf.

THE END